Hands off MY HONEY!

Jane Chapman

Tim Warnes

LITTLE TIGER PRESS
London

Bear **stomped** and **stamped** to his hollow by the **big oak tree.**

The ground **rumbled**. The daisies **shook** and the leaves **trembled** in the trees.

"I have a great big jar of delicious honey!" Bear bellowed. "And it is ALL mine!"

Bear looked around, but everyone had disappeared.

"Don't even **try** to take a **pawful!**" he boomed. "I am the **scariest bear** in the forest and I won't **share** a **single drop!**"

The woods were silent. Even the birds stopped chirruping. The only sound was the slurp of Bear's tongue as he licked.

"Mmmmmmmmm... yum yum..."

Mouse, the Rabbit Brothers and Mole
peered out of a bush.

"That jar is **enormous** and he's
keeping it all to himself!" whispered Mouse.
"Well, I **love** honey, and I'm going
to get some. Is anyone with me?"

The Rabbit Brothers both raised a paw.
Mole looked at the honey.
"I'm in."

Mouse picked her way carefully through the branches. The Rabbit Brothers held paws and began tiptoeing cautiously, when...

Snap!

"Whoopsie, that was me... on a twig," whispered Mole.

"Get down!"
hissed Mouse.

Bear's eyebrows lifted...
The animals held their
breath...

But Bear dipped his paw in
once more and was soon licking noisily.
"Phew," whispered Mole. "Sorry, Mouse."

Mouse patted him on the back.
"No harm done. Now, follow me."

Mouse zipped to the left and right, keeping to the shadows. The rabbits raced behind, shivering excitedly.

Mouse waved to Mole, but as he dodged a stinging nettle, he tripped over a root.

"Oooops!"

he squeaked.

Flump!

Bear turned suddenly...

Mole tucked his head
under his paws...

But
Bear
was busy
with a
long,
sticky
dribble
down
his arm.

"Sorry," whispered Mole. "Roly-poly Moley, eh?!"

Mouse peered through the ferns.
"Listen up, team," she whispered.
"We need to be **fast** and **silent** if we're
going to get that honey. Rabbits,"
she commanded, "lead the way."

The Rabbit Brothers and Mouse were masters at thorn dodging.

They **whizzed through** the brambles and

pole-vaulted over the puddle.

Taking a deep breath, Mole
headed into the thorns.
A prickle stuck in his
bottom, but he didn't
even squeak.

"I can do this!" thought Mole.
"I'll leap over the puddle, and finish
with a commando roll on the grass!"
He picked up a stick and
began to run.

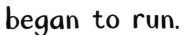

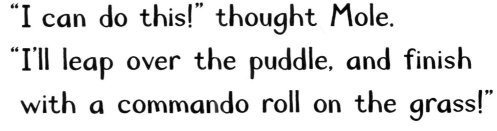

Splash!

"Oh no! Just look at me!"
gasped Mole. "I'm soaking!"
The Rabbit Brothers
clung to each other.

Mouse froze.

Bear's slurping stopped.
Bear's ears twitched.
Bear's eyes popped.

"What's going on here?"

he growled.

"Oooooh… Mouse said she **loves** honey and she's going to get some!" cried Mole from the puddle.

"**What? Didn't you hear me say this honey is mine?**" roared Bear.

"Yes, I did!" Mole squealed.
"But Mouse said SHE was going to… Oh! Look!"

Mouse slowly stretched out her arm and dipped it in the honey jar. She scooped out a golden pawful and licked her fingers triumphantly.

"Ooooooh!" cried Mole, covering his eyes. "I can't look!"

Bear swung Mouse up in the air … and they both laughed and **laughed.**

Bear rolled the Rabbit Brothers over in the grass and tickled Mole's tummy and toes.

"You win **again!**" he laughed. "You're all just too quick for me!"

The wriggly, giggly heap of paws and whiskers got stickier and stickier. "**Big Scary Bear** is my **favourite** game!" sighed Mole happily. "Can we play it again, **please?!**"

"Oh all right," smiled Bear, standing up.

"You lot go and hide...